STYLE RULES!

For my two fresh princesses, Mari and Lila, who taught my heart to sing—D.M.

To the AMAZING Christy, because sometimes making your mark means waiting for the perfect timing. Thank you!—G.J.

Fresh Princess: Style Rules!
Copyright © 2020 by Treyball Content, LLC
All rights reserved. Printed in the United States of America.
No part of this book may be used or reproduced in any manner whatsoever without written permission except in the case of brief quotations embodied in critical articles and reviews. For information address HarperCollins Children's Books, a division of HarperCollins Publishers, 195 Broadway, New York, NY 10007.
www.harpercollinschildrens.com

Library of Congress Control Number: 2019910790
ISBN 978-0-06-288458-9

The artist used Adobe Photoshop to create the digital illustrations for this book.
Design by Chelsea C. Donaldson
20 21 22 23 24   PC   10 9 8 7 6 5 4 3 2 1
❖
First Edition

FRESH PRINCESS

STYLE RULES!

Written by Denene Millner

Illustrated by Gladys Jose

HARPER

An Imprint of HarperCollins*Publishers*

Destiny is super excited because, just like a Fresh Princess should, she loves, loves, loves school.

Though she still misses her old friends, she's been imagining all the newness:

A new teacher (she'll be really nice).

New classmates
(they'll be really fun).

A cool new playground (swings are her jam).

And the most exciting of all: riding the bus to school
with everyone from the block.

There's only one thing Destiny isn't too thrilled about: her new uniform.
The straight skirt.
The white shirt.
And the pea soup—colored jacket.

Let's just say the Fresh Princess is not a fan. All of it is a snore, except for the jacket lining.
It has some promise.

Her mom and dad get Destiny and her sister, Marley, super pumped for their new experience. "Your school will be great. Just remember: have fun, do your best, and make your mark," her mom says.

Still, Destiny goes to bed a little nervous.
How will she stand out?

The next morning, her dad makes his famous first-day-of-class feast: waffles, eggs with cheese, grits, and bacon. Always, there's extra honey to make the day sweet.

When the bus pulls up, Destiny's new school is
even bigger than she'd imagined.

She's glad she at least has her friends from the block.
They waste no time getting busy.

THE PAUL ROBESO
PREPARATORY ACADEM
OF ARTS & SCIENCE

Esete is a hall monitor. She wears a really cool vest.

Zoe is a helper in the lunchroom.

Mari reads the school announcements over the loudspeaker.

All are already making their mark. Destiny wonders how she will do the same.

Esete takes Destiny to her new classroom.

"Welcome! It's going to be a great year!" her teacher, Ms. Marberry, says. "Look at your beautiful twists!"

Destiny beams.

POETRY CLUB
meeting
hen: After school
here: Library

After the class settles in, Ms. Marberry gets down to business. "Okay, my amazing students. Who read at least ten books this summer?"

Destiny's hand shoots up. "I read seventeen," she says.

"Impressive! You're going to have a great year—I can feel it," Ms. Marberry says.

Out on the playground after lunch,
Destiny jumps rope,

climbs the monkey bars,

and finally gets a turn on her favorite,
the swing.

When the whistle blows, everybody rushes back inside. Destiny is in such a hurry, she doesn't notice right away she put on her uniform jacket inside out. It's so cute! She decides to leave it that way.

"Cool jacket," says Mari.
"Yeah, really cool," agrees Zion as he and the other students admire the jacket's colorful swirls.

Romy is not impressed. "You're not allowed to wear your jacket inside out," he insists. "You're going to get in trouble."

Destiny quickly turns her jacket back to its proper side. The not-so-fresh side. The last thing she wants is to make her mark by getting into trouble.

Later that night, Destiny thinks about what Romy said. She feels a little sad. Destiny knows just the person who will make her feel better.

"What's up, Fresh Princess?" Marley asks. She makes time for Destiny even though she is busy recording her podcast.

Destiny is quiet. Finally, she tells her sister how she almost got into trouble.

"I wasn't trying to break the rules," Destiny says. "I was just being myself."
Marley asks, "Well, do the rules say you can't wear your jacket inside out?"

Suddenly, Destiny's eyes light up. "Wait!" she says. "I was still wearing my
uniform, so I didn't do anything wrong."

Destiny is right!
She decides right then and there that she will wear her jacket inside
out, no matter what Romy or anyone else has to say.
When she gets dressed the next morning, that's exactly what she does.

Her dad notices first. "You sure look fresh, Fresh Princess!"
Her friends from the block think so, too.
And by the time she climbs off the bus, they're showing off
their colorful jacket linings also.

By lunchtime, even more students are whispering and turning their jackets inside out.

And after swinging on the swing and crossing across the monkey bars and double dutching and playing hopscotch on the pavement, everybody on the playground turns their jackets inside out—just like Destiny's.

The whole playground is a sea of colors and swirls!

"Well, don't you all look fancy," Ms. Marberry says as everyone walks into class behind Destiny. "Whose idea was this?"

The class gets quiet.

Really quiet.

Destiny shrinks a little in her seat. This is definitely
not the mark she was looking to make at school.

But even still, she finds the courage to slowly raise her hand.

Ms. Marberry smiles. "How clever of you, Destiny! You're wearing your uniform and looking mighty cool doing it."
Destiny breathes a sigh of relief.

"Tell you what," Ms. Marberry continues. "How about we make Wednesday Inside Out Uniform Day?"
The classroom buzzes with excitement. Destiny's smile is as wide as the colors on her jacket are bright.

And in that moment, being exactly who she is—smart, colorful, original, confident—is the perfect mark for Destiny to make. The freshest of all.